CABIN FEVER

SHORT GETAWAY ROMANCE

Susan Kiley

H S L
media

Cabin Fever is a work of fiction. Any resemblance to actual events or persons, either living or deceased, is purely coincidental.

ISBN 978-1-949588-09-5 (Trade Paperback)
ISBN 978-1-949588-10-1 (eBook)

Printed in the U.S.A.
Cover Design: Armend Meha
Editor: Susan Kiley
Interior Design: Maria Foster
Cover photo: depositphotos-stokkete

First HSL Media Printing, September 2018

Explore the world, hear the music, and find love in a cabin.

A Note from Susan

Thank you for picking a copy of *Cabin* Fever either from Amazon, Kindle, or a local bookstore. I appreciate your support. I hope you fall in love with Andrea and Jason's story.

Stick around to the end, I've included excerpts from *Love Struck,* and *Crossed Up.* Grab your favorite cold glass, snuggle into your favorite chair, and enjoy.

Happy reading,
Susan Kiley XO

P.S. Please be sure to sign up for my newsletter (**susanrkiley.com/newsletter**) so you don't miss out on any new book release announcements.

Titles by Susan Kiley

Motivational / Self-Help

A Resilient Soul

Never Lose Faith: Strength for The Journey

Extraordinary Ways to Simplify Your Life

A Writer's Guide

Novels

Someday

Short Romances

Love Struck

Crossed Up

Pleasure Island

Kissing Cousins

Young Readers Series

Words on a Page-Co-Authored, by Brianna Kiley

Rumor Has It

CABIN FEVER

by Susan Kiley

PROLOGUE

ANDREA PLUCKED THE STRINGS of her acoustic guitar, worn with age and a heart sticker on it, her feet resting on the bus seat in front of her. She hummed to herself, watching the darkness pass by her window. Being the only rider on the midnight bus, she had her choice of seats; she chose one in the back. She wanted to live a week secluded in the mountains—no distractions—a week to find her music.

For months, she struggled to finish her next *hit* song. The recording company she worked for, Great Hill Records, pushing her to pump out songs, but none of them felt right. Even though the record company decided she wouldn't sing the songs she wrote, she wanted each song to have meaning.

As an up-and-coming artist, the pressure to have a hit song was significant. The record company had plastered her face on billboards and television commercials for months, then the attention disappeared. If she didn't produce a *hit* song soon, her career in the music industry, nothing but a memory. This twenty-five-year-old loved to travel, so sneaking off to Canada was an easy decision.

Writing songs has, was, will always be her passion. With her inspiration gone, she needed a change of scenery. *Needed* didn't come close to describing the hunger and sharp bite of desperation speeding her fingers across her guitar on that warm September night. Just as the bus was empty of occupants, Great Hill Records was growing empty of patience. And, at this moment, Andrea needed a song.

She had packed her guitar and escaped without warning to an Airbnb cottage near a mountain in a small town in Canada.

CHAPTER ONE

THE BUS ARRIVED AT ITS STOP, and Andrea put her guitar back in its case before collecting her small suitcase out of the overhead compartment. A week getaway to Canada was Andrea's last shot at finding her voice.

She smiled at the driver and stepped off the bus. The dirt road spewed dry clay beneath her leather boots as she marched toward her week of inspiration. The secluded cottage appeared abandoned.

Andrea drew in a breath, pulled back her shoulders, and wrapped her hand around the one last family member she loved, Thelma. Up the steep hill, she saw the house where she'd call home for the next week, surrounded by trees and a flower decorated balcony to view the town at the base of the mountain.

She drew in another cleansing breath. She reached behind her head and released the large clip that held her long brown hair in a messy bun. Running her hands through her hair, she ruffled it and skipped to the doorstep.

The two-story house was quaint with white vinyl siding, and small windows on each wall. She stepped onto the porch and looked under the black mat for the key. Confused when it wasn't there, she turned the doorknob and swung the door open. "That's odd," she said.

Andrea swept into the house, dropping her bag and guitar, and kicking the door closed behind her.

"Hello? Anyone here?" she called out.

In front of her was a joint kitchen and living room with a staircase between them leading to the bedrooms and master bathroom. Several candles flickered and a faint masculine smell tickled her nose. She shrugged and locked the door. "What a way to welcome guests."

She clicked her tongue and walked to the kitchen island to look through the sliding glass door to a landscaped paradise, including an outdoor kitchen and fire pit. "The internet didn't come close to capturing the beauty." A smile reaching each eye spread across her face.

She wandered around the couch and coffee table, then opened a side door that led to the garage. She saw a black Mercedes parked in the lot and whistled with amazement. "The description never said they'd have a car for me to drive. I will give them a superior rating." She closed the door and returned to the kitchen to check the contents of the refrigerator.

A loud crash from upstairs filled the quiet house. Her heart stopped. She inched towards the first landing in between the sets of stairs. "Hello?" she called out, taking each new step with caution.

When she reached the top, she passed the bathroom door as a tall, well chiseled man wearing nothing but a white bathrobe came out. She screamed and turned to him with her fists at eye level ready to fight. Andrea stared at his cobalt eyes, black hair, square jaw, and the freckles that dotted his cheeks.

"Watch where you're walking," he said with a mixture of concern and confusion in his voice. "That's a good way to hurt your pretty face."

"You must be the owner," she said, breathing out her relief. "There was a loud noise, I thought it was an intruder."

He tilted his head to the side. "Are you the owner? My name's Jason Rutter." He held out his hand for her to shake, but she ignored it.

She scrunched her eyebrows and stood straight with her arms crossed. "No, I'm not. If I'm not the owner, and you aren't the owner, then that makes you an intruder."

Cute but crazy Jason thought. Oddly enough, it did nothing to diminish his attraction to her. "Try again, doe-eyes."

Her body tensed. "What the *hell* are you doing here?" Andrea said. "Start talking or I'm calling the police. I've rented this cottage and nowhere in the contract was there mention of a half-naked guy. Not that that's a bad thing in most situations, but in mine, no thank you. I want peace and quiet. No distractions. No annoyances."

Jason smiled. "I used one of those services to rent this place for a few days to relax. I could say the same thing." He leaned against the wall in the hallway, crossed his arms and allowed the cotton robe to open and show his distracting chiseled chest.

"That you would prefer a half-naked guy?" Andrea said. "I rented it for the week, now get out."

He wiggled his eyebrows. "You enjoying the view?"

"I was until you stepped into the hallway."

She was a few seconds ago. The thought of a sexy guy occupying the same space in a secluded cabin crossed her mind. Andrea drove the thought from her mind, replacing it with the reason she rented the cottage in the first place. "My cottage for a week. Get dressed and out of the house. I'm calling the police."

He laughed. "Okay, call the police, doe-eyes. In the meantime, let's get to know each other."

"No thank you."

"You from California?" Jason asked.

"None of your business," she said.

Apparently, she had issues—of the male species, and she looked to be stubborn. Still, it was an innate character flaw of his to annoy the hell out of women who were stubborn. She had no idea who she was up against.

"These aren't difficult questions, doe-eyes. I'm from Hollywood, don't you recognize me?"

"Nope. There are hundreds of *boys* in California."

"Oh doe-eyes, I'm no boy. I'm a movie director and my home is under renovations. I needed new scenery, fresh air, and a quiet place away from people to recharge my batteries."

Andrea raised her eyebrows, fighting the urge to laugh. "Someone's full of himself. I'm not familiar with the name, Jason Rutter."

CHAPTER TWO

HIS FACE TURNED RED, and Andrea's smile widened. "Are you kidding me? My father is one of the greatest movie directors in the history of Hollywood. I'm more of the Indie film genre. I prefer to promote independent screenwriters and help them focus their story to become a masterpiece. My biggest project was *Walking to the Moon*. It came out last year, and the reviews were tremendous. I read an interview that said Spielberg said he would never match my success."

She snorted. "And?"

Jason looked at her, but she returned his elated gaze with a blank stare. "I heard words coming out of your mouth, but it sounded like one of those Peanuts characters from Charlie Brown. Why don't you get back in that Mercedes in the garage and return to your Hollywood mansion?"

He was hooked. She was all type of feisty. The thought of red-spiked heels flashed through his mind.

"That car isn't mine," he said, "I prefer apple candy red Lamborghini's."

Andrea's eyes widened. "Yup, a Hollywood *boy*. This is my cabin for the week. You can leave now." She took a step toward the stairs, but Jason grabbed her wrist.

"Listen, doe-eyes, I arrived an hour ago. I was here first. I'm not leaving the cabin because a sassy girl with a cute smile asked me to leave."

Andrea jutted out her bottom lip, batting her eyelashes, and in a high-pitched tone, she said, "Ah, please, Mr. Director. If I sleep with you, will you give me the lead in your next movie?"

Jason nodded. "Will you wear spiked red heels?"

Andrea's head jerked back and her eyes bulged like a frog startled. "What type of movie director are you, a Cinemax one?"

His eye brows wiggled. "You're being facetious, but that's only happened once... well, five or six times. Those are fun movies."

"Pathetic. Ooh, facetious. You know big words, Hollywood?"

"Oh, the things I know." He rolled his bottom lip between his teeth, then released. "Guess how many scripts I've read, and I'm only twenty-eight."

"Don't care."

Jason laughed. Doe-eyes might be a stubborn frog, but so far, she'd shown herself to be quick and witty. His gut told him she was possibly the feistiest women he's met in years, but beyond that a good person. The Hollywood women he'd spent time with getting to know better only wanted one thing, and doe-eyes didn't seem to care about his credentials. And Jason generally went with his instincts.

"Do you know how successful that makes me?" he said. "Spielberg couldn't do what I've done at this age."

She rolled her eyes and pulled her arm away. "I'm not leaving, and if you don't either, there will be hell to pay." Stomping her feet one stair at a time, she stomped across the living room grabbed her suitcase from the front door and dragged it up the stairs with her.

Jason watched her, shaking his head, and laughing. Doe-eyes had balls. He appreciated that about her. And, now, she could be exactly what he needed.

"Doe-eyes, we got off on the wrong foot," he said, as Andrea charged toward him. "You got the dates wrong. It happens. Why don't I call the owners?"

Andrea's arm nudged his side as she passed him on her way to the master bedroom. "You do that while I get comfortable in *my* bedroom."

"You go do that," he said, pulling his cell phone out of his pocket. "Wait, no!" He shook his head and raced to the bedroom door. Andrea was tossing his clothes out of the tall dresser pushed in the corner and replacing them with her own. "Stop," he said, picking up a sweater to refold it and return it to its place in the drawer.

Andrea beamed with each piece she removed. "How much did you bring? Are you moving in here?"

Not waiting for a reply, she continued dumping his clothes and replacing the empty spots with hers. The movie director was flat-out gorgeous with a capital G. A dark-haired, gray-eyed, chiseled kind of gorgeous.

"I didn't know what to pack. I've never been to Canada," he said. "Doe-eyes, can you stop for a second? Let's work out a compromise."

Andrea stopped and turned on her heel to face him without staring. The white robe hung from his broad shoulders, his wet hair tousled.

"Stop referring to me as a woodland creature and I'll consider working out an agreement."

He extended his hands in front of him as if preparing to defend against an attack. "Okay, what should I call you?"

"Andrea."

"Andrea what?"

"None of your business, Hollywood. Nothing else you need to know." She pulled her eyes away from his seductive stare and turned her attention to organizing the dresser.

"Andrea none of your business, your mother must have hated you?"

She froze. "My mother is none of your business either," she said. "None of your business means none of your business."

"As you wish, doe-eyes," he laughed. "I'm only here a few days. After that, the cabin, including this bedroom, is yours."

Jason crossed his arms at his chest and kicked one of his feet over the other. He tilted his head to observe the five feet of feisty sexiness organizing her clothes. "Nothing to say, doe-eyes?" Jason said.

"Andrea."

"Okay, Andi."

She shook her head. "My name is Andrea. Where do you plan on sleeping?"

"There's a *guest* room across the hall. I'll help you unpack your stuff in there, *Andi*."

"HA!" she said, hopping onto the bed, then flopped back, arms spread on the two quilts. "It's too die for. I love the luxuriating feel of my bed."

Jason moved closer to Andrea and the bed. She stretched her arms and yawned. "Famous people don't always get their way. You should've learned that by now, Hollywood."

"Oh, I've learned that you don't get what you want… You take what you want," he said. "I should have known a simpleton like you wouldn't understand the Hollywood life." He moved a step closer to the bed, pretending to scroll through his phone.

"Simpleton?" She laughed. "If you must know, I'm a singer-songwriter for Great Hill Records. Believe me when I say *I understand* the pressures of Hollywood."

"Oh? Aren't you starting late in the business? What songs have you written?"

"I'm twenty-five, that's not considered late. I'm not allowed to say the names of the people I sell my songs too. The record company owns the rights. You should know all about legal stuff, Hollywood."

"So, that means you're not telling the truth. I bet you carry a guitar around for show." He jumps on the bed, she flops and lands caddy-whompas on the edge. His half-naked body fills three-quarters of the king-sized bed draped in two handmade quilts.

She squealed. "What the Sam heck!"

"Bed. Mine. First. Deal." Jason closes his eyes as a wide smirk covers his face.

"No, that's not fair," Andrea said. "It's my cottage."

Jason shrugged. He knew he had to make a tactical decision until he learned more about the sexy songwriter lying next to him.

Jason opened his eyes. "What do you say we share the bed?"

"I don't need the fame like you do. Believe me or not. I don't care," she said. "Why don't we... share?"

"You. Me. Share." He said his words in a low tone and wiggled his eyebrows.

As she watched him, her stomach flipped in knots. "Sure, why not. You can have the end of the bed. I'll picture you as my cute puppy." She grinned and with all her might shoved him closer to the side of the bed.

He didn't want to push back too hard, so he slipped off the bed. Glaring at her, she winked. He grinned and grabbed her suitcase. "You can have the bed, but I get your stuff."

"No!" she squealed again, shuffling off the bed. She lunged after him as he cradled her suitcase in his arms. Andrea clawed at her stuff, but he kept turning in circles to keep it out of her reach. "Give me my stuff!" She hopped onto his back and flailed her legs.

"Is that all you got, doe-eyes?"

"Don't call me that!" Andrea pounded on his head with her palm as he backed into the bed. He shook her off, and she collapsed on the bed. "Oomph! Fine. Why don't we switch on and off or something?" she asked, straightening her shirt, and running her fingers through her hair. "You're leaving soon, so you take the first night."

"Ah, so doe-eyes can compromise," he said, placing her suitcase on the mahogany chest at the end of the bed. "Now, do you want to watch me get undressed or should I give you a chance to leave?"

He untied the rope on the robe, and Andrea covered her eyes, screaming. "You're disgusting!" Looking through the slits in her fingers, she ran out of the room and down the stairs. Once in the living room, she collapsed belly first on the couch.

Andrea couldn't help a little smile. "He's *some* man." Her head raises until her eyes reach her guitar case she left next to the front door. "Don't worry, baby," she said to her guitar, "I won't let that man get in our way."

CHAPTER THREE

AFTER A FEW MINUTES, she felt her eyes get heavy and the cold leather cushions became warm. She snuggled into the corner seat and let a yawn escape her lips. She fell asleep. "I wear satin pajamas, but I forgot to pack them," he called out as he ran down the stairs. Jason strolled into the living room in his boxers with a shirt. He stood watching the rise and fall of her breathing. "I guess you'll take the couch."

He turned to ascend the stairs, then looked at Andrea over his shoulder. Grumbling to himself, he stomped back and scooped her into his muscled arms. He struggled to keep her still as she squirmed, her legs hanging limp and one hand flapping in his face. When he entered the bedroom, he placed her in bed under the quilts. He felt creepy watching her, but he couldn't take his eyes off her. "You're twenty shades of feisty, Andrea."

The next morning, Andrea shot upright and looked around, forgetting where she was. She parted the hair hanging in her face, then saw a blow-up mattress on the floor with a blanket tucked under the edges and a flimsy pillow at one end. Andrea bit her lip, wondering who this guy was. Slipping out of bed, she walked downstairs and saw Jason in jeans and a t-shirt, flipping pancakes in a frying pan as she turned the corner.

"Good morning," she said, sitting at the round table in a chair by the wall. In front of the table was the kitchen island, surrounded by the standard top of the line kitchen appliances and cupboards hanging on the walls. It was five times the size of the kitchen in her apartment.

"Do you want pancakes?" he asked. "Or are you the girl that doesn't eat carbs?"

"I don't like pancakes. I'll have cereal."

The frying pan clattered on the stove. He looked at her with his mouth open.

"What?" she asked. "Do you want me to throw you a dog biscuit?"

"How do you *not* like pancakes? That's a sin."

"There's no flavor to them," she said, picking an apple out of the fruit bowl in front of her.

"That's what the syrup is for!"

"Then why not just eat syrup?"

"Because that's disgusting, doe-eyes."

"What did we talk about last night?" She glared at him as she sank her teeth into the apple with unnecessary force.

"Sorry, *Andrea*," he said, shuffling pancakes onto a plate and drowning them in maple syrup. He plopped the plate on the table across from her and stabbed his fork into the stack. Cutting a small piece, he shoved it in her face. "Try my homemade recipe." Syrup dropped into the fruit bowl, and Andrea sighed.

"I don't like them. End of story."

"Well, then you don't like me," he said with feigned hurt. "This is my special vanilla and almond extract recipe."

"You're right, I don't like you," she said, "since you're trying to kill me. I'm allergic to almonds."

"Even the extract?" he said, shoving the pancakes in his mouth.

"The extract is worse." Andrea stood and grabbed the jug of milk from the fridge to have Cheerios for breakfast. After pouring the milk, she rested her elbows on the island and stared at him while he continued to shove pancakes into his mouth. Stirring the cereal to make it soggy, she asked, "Why did you come out here?"

"I needed a getaway," he said with his mouth full. "You know, a secluded getaway away from people." Jason had scarfed his large stack of pancakes before Andrea dipped her spoon into her cereal. He dropped his dishes into the sink and leaned against the counter, standing beside her. "You?"

"I think you're lying," she said, scooping Cheerios out of the bowl. "What kind of Hollywood director comes to a secluded house in Canada just to relax? Aren't there, like, a million spas you can go to?"

"But then I wouldn't have met such a *feisty* girl like you," he retorted, "in a secluded cabin in the mountains of Canada. Alone."

Andrea gulped. "Fine, don't tell me," she said, dropping her half-eaten breakfast into the sink. "I nominate you for dishes," she shouted as she exited the kitchen.

She returned to the kitchen with her guitar case and went outside to sit in the grass near the large spruce tree with robust needles. Leaning against the guitar case, she rested her guitar in her lap and strummed out of tune chords. "I knew the cold bus would get to you, Thelma," she whispered to her guitar.

Thelma a replica 1969 Martin N-20 with a Baldwin pickup, the same guitar Willie Nelson has played for decades. Thelma has been beside Andrea since her eighth birthday when her aunt gave it to her. Since then, Thelma's never left Andrea's side. Thelma was her only family.

Jason watched her fiddle with the tuning, holding his mug of coffee. He poured a second cup and brought it outside. "Coffee?" he asked, resting the cup on her closed case. "Unless you're allergic to that too?"

She stared up at him through the strands of hair falling in her face. "Can you not be out here? I'm trying to focus."

He sat across from Andrea, cross-legged, and handed her the cup. "Drink coffee to destroy the grumpy monster in your stomach. My mom used to say to my dad all the time, not that it worked."

"Are you going to talk about your dad the whole time you're here? I get it, you're all so famous no one's heard about any of you, especially you."

He shrugged. "Only those who claim to be songwriters and wanna be singers," he said. "I'd rather talk about myself. I'm way more fascinating than my dad."

"Then, tell me why you're here."

"I already did."

"Not really, but whatever."

Jason placed the second coffee cup on the guitar case and finished his before resting his palms behind him and stretching out his legs. "I'm here to relax."

"Because you have such a tough life, Hollywood boy." She strummed more chords, now tuned, and hummed to herself.

"I think I know you," he snapped.

Andrea stopped playing and breathed. "Must you be so annoying?"

"I'm sorry, are you talking to yourself?"

"Ha, ha." She rolled her eyes and kept plucking the strings.

"I think… I mean you look familiar." He snapped and sat up straighter. "Now that I think of it, you look like that singer who overdosed last year. What was her name? Jodie… something or other."

Andrea clenched her jaw and hugged her guitar, staring at the ground. "Jodie Bloom. That was her stage name, anyway."

"Jodie Bloom! That's it! She was the hottest country artist on the charts for months on end. You wouldn't believe how the album sales skyrocketed when news of her death spread. It was such a tragic story. I heard they'll be doing a documentary on her death soon."

"It won't happen without permission of her family," she said through gritted teeth.

"I don't think she had any family," he said, picking lint off his shirt.

"She did."

"Really? I never saw anything in the articles I read."

"Don't believe everything you read, Hollywood," Andrea said. "She had me."

Jason's face turned white as he stared at her cold, brown eyes. "Her niece…"

"Yeah, she and my mom were identical twins, but Jodie raised me when my mom disappeared. Jodie struggled with addiction her whole life, but she loved me. When she passed, I got a pitiful allowance from my inheritance. Jodie's attorney placed everything into a trust. I don't get control over the trust fund or the royalties until I'm thirty. Who chooses an age like thirty, anyway? I had no one and an empty bank account."

"What about your dad?"

"He was never in the picture. Jodie was my only role model." Andrea sniffed and wiped away a tear.

"Andrea, I'm sorry. I didn't know." He reached forward to touch her hand, and she swatted it away.

"We don't know each other, so don't pretend to be my friend," she said, packing up her guitar, knocking the coffee in the grass. "I'll be in the bedroom for the rest of the day, and you can have every other part of the cottage to yourself. Just leave me alone." Andrea stormed off, leaving Jason speechless.

Later that day, Andrea laid in bed with her guitar on her stomach. She sang about things she saw in the room but never found inspiration for a real song. Then, there was a knock on the door and Jason came in. "I'm sorry for earlier."

"No, I'm sorry," she said, sitting up with her guitar.

"I didn't mean to intrude on your personal life." He sat on the edge of the bed, afraid to speak again.

"I lashed out for no reason. None of that is your fault. Let's forget about it. We can cohabitate. What do you say?"

Jason rested his hand on top of hers, both feeling a tingling sensation on their skin. "I made you lunch. Care to join me?"

"Sure, but I should change my clothes first. I've been wearing this since yesterday."

"To be honest, I haven't made anything since I thought you would decline," he said. "Why don't you go shower and I'll make us sandwiches with chips?"

"Wow, what a beautiful empty gesture," she said, rolling her eyes. Walking to the master bathroom, she stopped at the door and looked over her shoulder. "This lunch better be worth it. I don't get dolled up for a guy I met two seconds ago."

Jason grinned. "Technically, we met yesterday."

"Technically, we argued."

"Technically, I won," he said.

"Technically, I did. Who slept on the couch and who slept in a luxurious bed?"

"Touché. But who smells better?" He waved his hand in front of his nose and cringed. Andrea waved him off and entered the bathroom. "I'm sure you look beautiful no matter what you wear," he whispered as she closed the door.

Jason returned downstairs and made them BLTs for lunch with sliced apples and a garden salad as a side. He sat at the table when he finished with his presentation and rested his elbows on the edge. He waited ten minutes before she came down with her hair pulled into a ponytail wearing an ankle-length black skirt and a white blouse. Jason tried to pretend he didn't notice as Andrea sat across from him. "Feel better?"

"Yes," she said.

Jason smiled. "Smell better too."

Rubbing her hands together, she stared at the food and drooled. "I didn't realize how hungry I was until I smelled bacon." Gripping the sandwich with both hands, she took a huge bite. "Delicious."

"It's rude to talk with your mouth full."

"Says you!" Bits of the sandwich and saliva flew out at Jason. He swiped it off, while she covered her mouth and tried to avoid laughing. "I'm sorry," she said after swallowing.

"You seem to be in a better mood," he said, serving salad into her bowl, "I guess you needed a hot shower."

"I found my inspiration in there."

"Oh yeah? Did it give you *sexual healing*?"

"What? Ewe! No! Stop thinking sexual things about me." She grumbled to herself and picked the thickest apple slices off the plate. "I meant that I was thinking a lot about my aunt and wrote a song about how much pain I was in when she died."

"Can I hear it?"

She held still. "No."

"Oh."

She smiled. "I don't remember it anymore. I should thank you for inspiring me."

Jason wiggled his eyebrows. "So, you're thinking about me in the shower, huh?"

"Only to kill my sex drive."

"Seriously, though, how did I inspire you?"

Andrea crunched into an apple slice and smiled, her eyes squinting. "I guess being alone isn't what I needed. I had to get a new perspective. I've been thinking about you and your family dynamic, and how hard it must be to live in your father's shadow. I judged you too harsh, and all those thoughts got my creative juices flowing."

"I like when juices flow," Jason said.

He'd been joking, but she looked serious.

"That's kind of a compliment," he said with a shrug. "I'd like to continue being an inspiration for you."

"Do you think you'd stay here any longer if I needed a writing buddy?"

"I would if you asked me nice," he said, winking.

"Will you?"

Andrea felt her face warm and turned away so he wouldn't see her blush. "I think it would help my creative juices if you told me why you're here."

Jason shook his head, and his playful gaze turned serious. "I'm running away from my father, okay? My last movie bombed and I couldn't face the disappointment in his eyes. I needed to get somewhere far away from where I knew he wouldn't find me until he returns to Europe. Go ahead, make fun of me, I know that's what you're dying to do." He rested his arms on the table and dropped his head on them. "I'm a disgrace to the Rutter family."

Andrea reached over and patted the top of his head. "There, there."

Jason looked up with one eyebrow raised. "There, there?" He chuckled. "That's the best you can do?"

"What?" she shrugged. "I don't know how to console people. There, there seems standard."

"You're weird." He grinned, and Andrea blushed again.

"Weird is cool," she said, trying to reconcile what she thought she knew about Jason.

"Let's toast," Jason said, "to a partnership."

Andrea raised an apple slice. "To a partnership."

THAT EVENING, Andrea sprawled across the length of the couch with her feet in Jason's lap, both holding a glass of red wine. Some of it spewed out Andrea's nose as he finished a story about his first Hollywood actor run-in. "You zipped his fly up for him?" Andrea squealed, kicking her feet, "Without saying a word? You reached for it?"

"I was eight!" he protested, "I was the perfect height. My mom always did it for me, I thought people did that for each other."

"You were dumb at eight," she said, taking another sip of wine. "Well, you're dumb now, but that's boy DNA. Women are more sophisticated."

"Doe-eyes, I 'm no boy," Jason said. His wicked grin searing a hole into her heart. "So, you're telling me you wouldn't help a man in need if his underwear was about to display on national television?"

"I'd tell him, not do it for him." Andrea lifted her legs and pulled her knees into her chest. Her hair pulled over one shoulder and she wore an oversized sweater, pajama bottoms, and socks. Jason shuffled closer to her, resting his arm across the top of the couch. "If I hadn't come here, what would you be doing right now?"

"Oh, I don't know," he sighed, "bedding the locals and staking my claim to the land like the caveman I am."

"That's funny, I would have done the same thing."

They both chuckled, then silence fell between them. Andrea remained still while Jason pulled her beside him. "You know, you're beautiful when you're not talking."

Andrea gasped before slapping him with a pillow that sat on the armrest behind her. "You're a pig." She snorted imitating a pig but ended up making herself laugh.

Jason placed her wine on the table and pulled her along as he stood. She couldn't stay upright as she clutched her stomach. He held her right hand and wrapped his arm around her waist, placing her hand on his shoulder. They swayed to the sound of the whistling wind.

"What's happening?" Andrea whispered, placing her head on his chest.

"We're dancing. Enjoy the moment," he whispered, kissing the top of her head.

CHAPTER FOUR

ANDREA PULLED BACK AND dropped her arms. Jason bent, his lips seconds away from touching hers. "I think it's time for bed," Andrea said, pulling away and moving to the stairs. Changing her mind, she turned around again and planted a quick kiss on his tender lips before disappearing upstairs.

"Good night, doe-eyes," Jason mumbled watching her long legs and tight ass walk away before flopping onto the couch.

OVER THE NEXT FEW days, the two of them did their separate activities; Andrea played guitar and wrote songs while Jason ran on the dirt paths and watched television in the guest room. He hadn't slept in the master bedroom since the first night, wanting to give Andrea her space.

Aside from eating meals together and talking through the night on the couch or laying naked in bed, they existed as separate people. Andrea stole glances at him from across the room as she read a book while Jason picked flowers for her from the trails to put on the breakfast table in a vase.

On the day Jason was packing to leave, Andrea kept unpacking for him, putting his clothes back in the dresser next to her things. "Why can't you stay?" Andrea asked, "I like your cooking. I don't have to think about what to eat." She unfolded one of his sweaters and put it on. She grasped the collar and inhaled.

"I like your smell," exhaling as she twirled in front of the full-length mirror.

"Thanks."

She said, "Don't you want to relax in the grass and feel the clean Autumn breeze on your skin?"

Jason smiled and pulled the sweater off her. "I need to go back to work. My buddy Lawrence needs me to look at his new movie and shoot right away."

Andrea's bottom lip jutted before she plopped onto the bed in mock defeat.

Jason cocked his head to the side and said, "Besides, you need to keep working on your music and decide which song you will present to your manager. Isn't he worried about you?"

"No," she sighed, sitting on the side of the bed. "I told everyone I needed to get away and wouldn't be back for a while. I haven't checked my phone since I got here."

Jason grabbed her hands and kissed the back of one, then the other. "This was a fun adventure. I'm glad I got trapped here with you."

After several days with Andrea under the same roof, Jason was having a hard time imagining him not being there. Unfortunately, the cabin relationship remained nothing more than a partnership.

"Back at you," she said, pulling her hands away. Just as he was about to turn away, she jumped up and wrapped her arms and legs around him, squeezing him in a tight hug. "Thanks for being my inspiration," she whispered into his ear, leaving a wet impression with her soft lips, then let him go.

"You're welcome," he said, then finished packing in silence.

Andrea laid on the bed watching him until he had finished. He took his suitcases from the floor and turned to leave. "Do you think we'll run into each other in California?"

Jason rested against the doorframe, two suitcases in his hands. "Do you want to run into me?"

She shrugged. "Maybe just to insult you in your natural habitat. That would be fun."

"Are you sure, that's it?" Jason said. "Don't you think we should have a romp in the sack for the road?"

"Just get out of here!" she scowled, waving her hand at him. He made his way down the stairs, and Andrea fought the urge to run after him. She pulled her guitar in her lap to sing the song she'd written about him. Jason stayed in the living room until the music ended, then got in the waiting car and left.

AS HE DROVE THROUGH the quiet streets to the airport, the hook of Andrea's song played on a loop in his mind. Her flowing hair and sparkling eyes danced through his memories, her beautiful voice narrating the thoughts in his head. It didn't register he had reached the airport, entering the line to return rental vehicles.

Slapping the top of the back seat, he shouted, "Screw it! Turn around and go back." Stepping on the gas, the driver reversed before anyone could get in line behind him. Several cars honked as he navigated backward until he found a space to turn. Once he did, he sped along the highway back to the cabin. Jason sat in the backseat singing the lyrics he remembered from her song at the top of his lungs.

The driver parked in the driveway. Jason grabbed his suitcases then hopped the steps to the porch. With a huge grin on his face, he stood with his hands behind his back after ringing the doorbell. He heard the rustling in the living room, cursing himself for not stopping for flowers or chocolates.

The door opened and Andrea stood there in shock. "I put the key back under the mat," her eyes widened and her cheeks reddened, "You didn't have to ring the bell."

Jason was at a loss for words staring into her eyes. "I wanted… um… I wanted a more dramatic entrance." He stuttered, rubbing the back of his neck. They couldn't tear their gaze away from each other.

"Did you forget something? I was eating."

"I did forget something." Jason leaned against the doorframe and smiled. "I bet you made nothing as good as what I made."

Joyful tears filled Andreas eyes. "I microwaved leftovers from last night's dinner," she said. "Why are you here?"

"I told you. I forgot something," he said, wiping a tear away with his thumb. With that, he grabbed both her cheeks and planted a passionate kiss on her lips. Andrea fell into the moment. She hopped and wrapping her legs around his waist. He kicked the door closed and dropped her onto the couch before crawling on top of her.

Andrea couldn't help a big smile. "Did you find what you forgot?"

Jason eyed the shirt hugging Andrea's chest. He ran his hand the length of her body. "I did."

At that moment, everything else was invisible. Jason forgot his career duties and his father while Andrea couldn't think of a single lyric. She didn't have to, which was the stress relief she'd been looking for since the moment she got there.

Andrea pushed him to take off his shirt, and he did the same for her. By the time they reached the staircase, they were already in their underwear, naked when they made to the bedroom.

After they shared the warmth in the sheets, they both laid naked in bed, Andrea's head resting on his chest. The sky was dark, and the moon shined between the trees. Jason held her in his arms and kissed the top of her head.

"Why'd it take you so long to kiss me?" Andrea whispered. It was peaceful in the bedroom, it felt wrong to make unnecessary noise. The curtains flapped as the wind blew in through the open window, cooling off their heated bodies.

"Why is it on me?" Jason asked, running his fingers along her arm. His other hand rested behind his head as he stared at the curves her body made under the blankets.

"You're the big macho man. I assumed you wanted to make the first move."

Jason leaned against the headboard, letting her head fall to his thighs. "You mean to tell me we could have been having sex this whole time?"

Andrea scrunched her face. "Ewe, no. I hated you when I first saw you. I've been in California long enough to spot the pompous jerks."

"So, you were wrong about me?"

"I didn't say that," she said, lying in his lap with her nails trailing his thighs. Jason leaned over and kissed her lips. "I still think you're pompous with your work, but the jerk part is being tested."

Jason laughed. "How can you test it now? We slept together. I think it's clear you have positive feelings for me, and since I came back I'm not a jerk."

"It could have been angry sex."

"Was it?"

"No."

"Why did you come back?"

"For you."

"For me? Or for sex?"

Jason raised his eyebrows. "Is that how you want to play it?"

"Maybe," she said.

"We'll see." Jason put his hands on her sides and tickled her. She squealed, kicking her legs, and batting his hands away.

"Stop it!" she said, unable to say the words loud enough, "This. Hurts. Stop." She giggled until she escaped his grasp. She straddled him and pinned his wrists to the headboard. Kissing his nose, she said, "You should know," she took another swipe of his nose, "I always win."

"I'll let you keep thinking," he said, "you won while I continue to win too."

AT MIDNIGHT, the two of them showered together. After making out in the bathroom and dripping water everywhere, they were starving for a late snack. Jason wore only his boxers while his white robe draped over Andrea holding a cup of warm tea. She sat at the kitchen island while he cooked eggs. "I'm glad you came back," she said.

He looked at her over his shoulder. "Me too," he grinned, "I don't think I could have forgiven myself had I gotten on that plane."

"I hope your ticket was refundable."

Jason dismissed her comment with a wave of his hand. "No, but it's not a big deal. I've missed so many flights from partying too hard and sleeping with..." He paused, and cleared his throat, sending an apologetic look to Andrea.

"It's okay," she laughed, putting her mug in front of her, "I know you've slept with other women, and I'm not a virgin either. We're both adults here, and I'm not interested in drama. We came here to escape that, remember?"

Jason shuffled eggs onto the plate in front of her and she scooped a large fork full into her mouth. "That doesn't mean I need to talk about my countless conquests. I've had weekends with an endless chain of sex, sex, sex, sex. Who needs to hear any of those details?"

They smiled at each other, and she stuck her tongue out at him. "I 'm not the jealous type. Don't think you'll make me jealous with sex talk. I have you now and that's what counts."

"You do." He ran to the other side of the counter and scooped her into his arms, spinning her while he kissed her. When he let go, he ate his eggs sitting next to her, while playing footsie between the stools.

FOR THE NEXT FEW DAYS, their routine was the same: have sex, shower, eat, play cards, repeat.

Andrea found time in between to be alone with her music while Jason explored the different paths through the woods.

The bare bones of her song were there, but she still couldn't get the chorus right. Something kept her rooted until the song was perfect. Her manager tried to call and text, but she returned the same message: I'll return soon.

Andrea cruised into the kitchen late one afternoon after showering, Jason prepared the kitchen table.

"Are you ready to lose?" Jason said. "I love my prize."

Andrea nodded. "And I love losing." She took her seat opposite Jason at the table.

"Strip poker," he announced to Andrea. "Are you ready, doe-eyes?"

She rolled her eyes. "I guess. It's not like I've gotten any better since yesterday."

Jason shuffled the cards and dealt. First hand Jason won, Andrea lost her t-shirt. Jason smirked. "Looks like another win for Mr. Hollywood."

"I wouldn't be too sure of yourself, Hollywood," Andrea said. "You never know what tricks I have up my sleeves."

Jason grinned. "Appears none," he said. "since you lost your shirt already."

"Touché, Mr. Hollywood."

A couple more hands and a lot less clothing, they had played out. Jason sat across from Andrea in nothing but his boxers, and razzed Andrea about her monumental win.

Andrea sat with her clothed legs propped on the table top as Jason stared at her.

"So, how is it you were horrible all the other times?" Jason asked.

Andrea shrugged. "Beginners luck," she said.

Jason smiled. "Of course."

She removed her feet from the table and stood. "My aunt taught me how to play when I was ten." She moved to put the wine glasses into the dishwasher. "She learned from her mother when she was a kid," Andrea said. "I guess she thought it was a tradition she had to pass onto me."

"Hmm. You bamboozled me," Jason said.

He didn't like losing, but losing meant winning. Either way, he got exactly what he wanted—Andrea under the handmade quilts under his muscular body. "I'm ready to give you your prize," he said. "Are you ready to collect?"

She held still, and Jason moved in to give Andrea her prize.

CHAPTER FIVE

THE FOLLOWING EVENING, the sat outside in the grass on a blanket, drinking wine and eating cold pizza. "This is the perfect pairing," Andrea said, resting on his chest as she sat between his legs. "I think we should have this for dinner every night."

"You'd get sick of it fast," he said, nuzzling her neck, and smelling her strawberry-scented hair. "I heard you singing your song today. It sounds done. Can I hear it?"

She stilled. "No, I'm not ready for anyone to hear it yet."

"Why not?" he said and hummed the tune.

"Stop it," she grumbled, "It's not perfect yet."

"Why does it have to be perfect?"

"Because it has to make my aunt proud. This is the first song I've written since I signed my record deal. If it doesn't knock the producers off their chairs, what kind of artist am I? A one-hit wonder?"

"Never," he said, kissing her shoulder, "I can tell you have talent, doe-eyes, from the other songs you've played for me. You're getting too caught in your head. The point of coming here was to escape that."

"You think I don't know?" she scoffed, "I'm a failure if I can't make this work. It's too much pressure."

"So, quit."

"I can't quit."

"Stop whining."

"But…" Andrea frowned and batted her eyelashes at Jason, "Why are you being so mean?"

Jason cupped his hand around her chin and squeezed her cheeks together so her lips jutted out more. "You're so cute." He kissed her lips, and she slapped his hand away, stretching out her jaw and glaring at him. "Being angry makes you cuter," he chuckled.

"Your phone is ringing every five minutes," she said. "Why don't you answer it? Your ringtone is catchy. I want to dance when I hear it ring."

He smiled. "Then get up and dance for me," he said. "There were calls from my dad, friends, and business people wondering where I've been. Not important. I want to focus on you."

"You can call them back. I won't be mad or anything. We've had several days together."

He looked almost wounded. "Speaking of which, why don't we head back to the bedroom?" Jason said.

Andrea turned and faced him sitting cross-legged. "Why do you avoid your dad? Having a family is important. What if he needs you?"

"He doesn't need me. I know why he's calling," Jason said as he looked above her head. "He wants to tell me the next greatest success he's accomplished. He's competitive with me and it's rather childish."

"Maybe he's doing it to push you to be better than you are?"

"That's none of your business," he snapped, standing.

"Jason," she said, placing her hand against his thigh.

"I'm sorry, it's a bad topic." A grin crossed his face. "I'll race you to the bedroom. I call being on top."

Andrea crossed her arms, forcing herself not to laugh. "It's a warm night," she said with a serious expression. Jason stopped. "This might be the wine talking, but why don't we sleep out here?"

"We won't be doing much sleeping," he said, pulling her into a kiss. They slipped onto the blankets, undressing each other.

Andrea realized she had just committed a tactical error, because she didn't stop him from kissing her. And now another, because she was kissing him back.

She knew if they continued, they would make love under the stars. Telling herself she was fifty shades of crazy, Andrea deepened the kiss and touched the muscle on his chest. While they kissed more, he brought her tighter against his naked body.

"Aren't you going to do that magical thing with your fingers?" she asked. Because she really wanted him to.

He pulled away from her. "Hmm. I haven't made my mind up yet."

"And what can I do to assist you with making your mind up?"

She rolled her bottom lip between her teeth.

"One question," he said. "Will you do that thing with your nails?"

Andrea looped a strand of her hair behind one ear. "I think I can manage that."

Jason pulled Andrea into his warm beating chest before laying her on the blanket.

SUNRISE WAS AN HOUR AWAY. Still, Andrea couldn't sleep. Taking care not to disturb Jason peacefully sleeping half naked under the clear skies, Andrea padded across the lawn fresh with dew to the house.

Once the sun rose, Jason woke and Andrea wasn't beside him under the blanket. Her clothes sprawled across the grass, but she wasn't in sight. Moments later, she came outside in his bathrobe holding her guitar case. "Good morning, beautiful," he said with a croaky voice.

"Don't speak," she said, sitting by his head. "I will play you my song, then we'll never speak of it again. Do you understand?"

"I can't promise I won't freak out about how good it is," he said, kissing her knee. She scowled, and he laughed. "Okay, okay, I won't say a word."

Andrea nodded and took a deep breath. Her right hand held a pick that hovered over the strings while the fingers on her left hand fiddled to find the first chord.

When she strummed, the sound hit Jason with strong emotions, his sorrow brought forward. Then, she opened her mouth, and Jason felt more hopeful from the lyrics of the ballad. Her voice soft until her confidence rose. It was a song describing her aunt, without referencing her. Jason didn't understand why the song reflecting loss and coping with the truth affected him so much.

When the song ended, he was silent. They stared at each other, neither spoke. Jason's mouth hung open as she put her guitar back in the case. Without a word, she removed his robe, climbed on top of him, and they made love again before going inside.

CHAPTER SIX

ON A COOL AFTERNOON, Andrea and Jason cuddled next to each other on the couch with a blanket draped over them. They watched television while sipping wine and kissing during commercials. Jason stood, but Andrea pulled him. "I have to pee," he whispered.

"Fine," she huffed, "but get back here before I get cold." He laughed and walked upstairs. Andrea noticed his phone on the long table next to the couch. The screen lit and she leaned forward to see he had eighty-two missed calls from various numbers and a handful of voicemails. "Jason!" she called out, her hand hovering over the phone.

"I'll be back!"

"I think something's wrong."

"Yes, I had to leave you for a minute."

Andrea frowned at the phone. "Your phone's blowing up! I think you should see this."

Seconds later, Jason returned in his boxers. "I put it on silent for a reason."

Andrea handed him his phone, and he scrolled through the texts as he settled on his seat. Andrea looked at him as he tossed the phone to the other side of the couch and looked straight at the television. "Jason?"

"It's nothing."

"Jason."

"Don't look at me like that."

"How do you know how I'm looking at you?"

"I can sense it."

Andrea pulled herself into his lap, kissing his cheeks. "What were those messages? What happened?"

"It's nothing."

"Jason, don't play these games. We said no secrets, remember?"

Jason closed his eyes. "It's not a secret. I don't care."

"About what?"

"My dad died."

Jason pushed her off his lap and left to open another bottle of wine in the kitchen. Andrea followed him and wrapped her arms around his waist from behind. "I'm so sorry, Jason," she said, kissing his back, "I guess that means you're going back to L.A.?"

"Why?" He struggled to pull the cork out of the bottle, grunting.

Andrea hopped onto the counter to face him. "He's your dad. Don't you want to be with your friends and family? Arrange a memorial service? Mourn him with people who knew him?"

"No one knew him. He let no one in long enough to find out."

Andrea sat on the kitchen counter. She could sum up her state as confused and happy. She didn't understand all the dynamics of Jason and his family, but she wanted to because she was in love. She'd tried to hold her heart safe from Jason, but it had unlocked days earlier. Everything seemed happier and fitting, though she supposed that could be from the copious amounts of wine and sex, too.

"It's okay if you're pissed. Scream. Stomp," she said.

Jason closed his eyes again. "We never had the greatest relationship, and I bet my mother is maxing out her credit cards right now. That's how she celebrates.

There's nothing I can do about his death, so there's no need for me to rush home. I want to stay here with you."

"I want that too," she said, pulling him close, "but I understand if you must leave."

"I'm not leaving," he said, putting the bottle back in the fridge. He headed for the stairs, looking back to see if she was following. "Come on, Andrea," he said with a forced smile. "We haven't done it in the guest bedroom yet."

Andrea hopped off the counter, sauntering toward him. "Why haven't we done it there yet?"

Jason shrugged. "Oversight on my behalf."

"Totally your fault."

"We must regain lost time. Race you." Jason took two steps at a time on the stairs, while Andrea went slow, unsure of what to think.

CHAPTER SEVEN

THE NEXT DAY, THEY CONTINUED their usual routine, but the only difference, Jason was distant. The following afternoon, Andrea ruffled the tufts of hair hanging over his forehead, watching him sleep. He didn't sleep well the night before, and she knew better than anyone how badly losing a parent could affect someone. "I know how I'll cheer you up," she whispered, pressing her fist into her cheek as her elbow rested on the pillow, "If you don't want me to do it, speak. Jason. Jason."

Andrea smiled, planning the picnic she'd make in her head. Throwing herself out of bed, she ran to the kitchen, careful not to clang pots or slam cupboards. She put a cheese sandwich on the frying pan, washed grapes, and strawberries, and picked out her favorite white wine.

As she headed to the stairs to wake Jason, the smoke detector blared. "The grilled cheese!" she exclaimed, rushing to the stove to turn off the burner. She flapped away the smoke with a hand towel, and Jason rushed into the kitchen.

"What the hell!?" Jason said, as Andrea dumped the burned sandwich into the trash under the sink. "Are you okay?"

"Yeah." She stared at her failure, draping the towel over her neck, "I forgot the sandwich."

"Clearly," he said, hugging her, "Why didn't you wake me?"

"I wanted to surprise you."

He smiled. "Why don't we make lunch together?"

So, this is what it felt like to have a knight rush in and save the damsel in distress. She sniffled and thought this whole scene was possibly the funniest thing ever.

"You can make it. I'm useless. Can't even make a sandwich." Andrea watched his kind eyes before kissing his lips. She hated how whiny she sounded, so she changed her mind and cleaned her mess before helping Jason cut vegetables for his pasta salad.

"You're going to love it," he said, pouring rigatoni into a large pot. "My mother taught me how to make it when I was younger, and every girl I've made it for has fallen in love with me."

Andrea washed off the knife and placed it in the sink. "You want me to fall for you?"

"I only make this for special girls."

"Ahh, I'm special."

He smiled. "Very."

Andrea leaned in until her lips met Jason's. "As are you." She grabbed two plates from the cupboard. He squeezed her butt. "Did your mom teach you everything about cooking?"

Jason nodded. "Cooking together is the best memory I have with her. I never wanted to shop or get my nails done, so this was our thing."

"I'm happy you preferred food over manicures and glamour."

He laughed.

When lunch was made, it was too windy to picnic outside, so they moved the coffee table and laid out the blanket in the living room. Jason was quiet as they ate, while Andrea tried telling him knock-knock jokes and throwing bits of food at him to make him smile.

"Don't waste it," he said, looking out the window.

She shuffled closer to him and kissed his cheek. "Thanks for making lunch. I don't know how I would have handled the situation if the smoke alarm didn't go off. We could have been engulfed in flames. Once you're asleep, there's hardly anything that can wake you. I'm surprised the fire alarm was enough."

Jason said nothing as Andrea rambled. She smiled at him, and she found herself considering how it would feel to know more about his life prior to the cabin. She began to lean toward him, but the lean immediately followed by panic, and Andrea grabbed her drink and took a slow long sip. "We need to talk."

"Why?" He chewed on a grape tomato, avoiding her gaze.

For a moment, Andrea thought she'd not push him further. "Don't play coy. You know why."

Jason stretched his legs out while gazing into Andrea's eyes. "Look. He's my dad. He had a heart attack. People are calling me to check in. What else is there to say?"

Andrea scrunched her lips and sat cross-legged. "When my aunt died, I wanted to be alone. I pushed everyone away and told them I was fine. I didn't leave the house, and not even my manager wanted to get too close. I asked for space, and I got it, ten-fold. One night, I needed someone to talk to and I didn't know who I could call. I ruined a couple of friendships because of my grief, and I had a total breakdown because of my loneliness. My manager came over the next morning to find me completely hungover. I'd left him a bunch of voicemails that I don't remember, even when he played them back. Isn't it sad that I didn't have any girlfriends to comfort me? I had a man who was twice my age and the only other person who knew my aunt on the same level as me."

"What's your point?" Jason asked.

"You shouldn't be alone. Let your feelings out. I don't care how. Do it."

"I'm fine."

Andrea's eyes bulged from her face. "You're not! I know they say you're supposed to let people mourn in their own way and you can't rush it, but you haven't even started yet," Andrea said. She dipped her head before locking eyes with Jason. "I want you to go to California and be with your family and friends. I'm trying to help you."

"Did I ask?"

"You didn't have to." There was silence, then Andrea spoke without making eye contact. "Your dad died."

Jason shook his head.

Andrea raised from her place on the floor and stood in front of him. "Your dad died."

"Stop saying that."

"You say it," she said, leaning over, and shoving his chest. She moved two steps back and curled her fingers towards herself. "Stand and shout. Scream. Push me. Throw your cup. Do something."

He stood. "Why are you doing this?"

"I care about you too much to ignore this. Hit me."

"No."

"Hit me!"

"Andrea!" he said, finally yelling. He took a step forward, fists clenched and breathing heavily. Andrea looked at him solemnly, thinking he'd finally scream and throw things. Instead, he collapsed on the couch and buried his face in his hands. He sniffed and rubbed his eyes.

Andrea sat beside him, rubbing his back. He flinched at first, then welcomed it.

"I don't want to be upset," he said, "I want to be happy. I listened to my mom's voicemail earlier and she sounded ecstatic. She said she's happy that his drinking and drug use had caught him. She used to worry, even after their divorce. She paid for his rehab three times, which he never gave her any money, ever."

"You don't have to explain anything to me," she said, a sinking feeling in her gut, "I think I was wrong to push you. I'm sorry."

Andrea glanced away and then back to see Jason watching her. She was uncomfortable in these moments. She was unsure what to say next. She tilted her head. "Do you want me to leave or bring you something to drink or eat?"

"I think there's a charred sandwich in the trash," he said, trying to laugh. He looked at her with longing, and pulled her into his arms. "I meant what I said before. I want to be with you. I don't want to go back there, facing the people and stares. I can't fake sadness for a father who was never there for me. He spent more time on his career."

"Okay, Jason, whatever you want," she said touching the side of his face with her hand.

"I know his funeral is going to be a party. People will say things to please the paparazzi. The guests will pretend they hate it, but they love the publicity and pretending to mourn for someone they didn't care for."

"You don't know it will be like that."

"It will," he said, stroking Andrea's hair. "His current wife loves being in the spotlight. She'll make sure everyone sees her being the grieving widow, trying to hide the dollar signs in her eyes. She'll control every detail of the party, making sure my dad remains in the public eye to make money off his death. That's always the way, isn't it? Someone dies, and sales soar. This must be déjà vu for you. Why don't we go for a walk?"

Andrea stared at the uneaten food on their makeshift picnic in the living room. "A walk will be good for you. I'm sorry for pushing."

"Don't give it a second thought," he said, wiping his cheeks with the sleeve of his shirt. He stood to clean the mess, but Andrea grabbed his hand and pulled him back.

"I'm here for you. Whatever you need. Whatever you decide to do, I will support you."

Jason kissed her lips. "I want to go for a walk and find a private place," he said with a wink.

"Adventurous," she said, looking concerned, "I like it."

The following days, they found 'private' places in the woods to act like Tarzan and Jane. Cabin fever raged as they found increased difficulty keeping their hands off each other while cooking, watching movies, or when Andrea played her guitar.

CHAPTER EIGHT

THE FOLLOWING NIGHT, ANDREA SAT IN BED reworking the lyrics of her song in her notebook, while Jason fondled her breasts and touched every inch of bare skin. "Stop it," Andrea giggled, resting against the headboard. "I'm trying to work. A few more lines and I'll be finished."

"And I've only begun."

Andrea shook her head. "I'm excited to share the song with the producers."

"That's good," he said, kissing her shoulder. "My mother called when you were in the shower."

"Oh, yeah?" she asked, trying not to mention his father by biting her tongue.

"Yeah… she was in tears she said. She was begging me to come home and take care of everything. Dad's wife went AWOL, so my mom is dealing with the paparazzi, reporter's questions, and planning the funeral."

"That must be hard for her. What are you going to do?"

Andrea sat thinking of the right words to say. Back when her aunt died, she tuned all the outside noise out. Now, as she looked at the man she'd fallen for, she saw how far removed from the Hollywood life he once lived. "I'm torn, but I know in my heart the correct thing," he said as he rested his head on her naked chest.

"Didn't your father have a manager? Even little me has a manager."

"Yes. Well, not anymore. His new wife fired everyone and she paid herself as my father's manager." Jason raised his head for a moment. "I'd rather not talk about Hollywood."

"Okay. But you never said what you're going to do."

"I should go home, even if I'd rather not." Jason raised his head under their eyes met. He kissed her nose. "I'd ask you to come, but I want you to finish your song first. I think I need to be with my family and focus on them."

Andrea nodded.

"But . . ."

"It's okay Jason, I understand."

His eyes met hers. "You know it's not what I really want, right?"

"Yes," she said, but felt hurt. "You do what you have to do." Jason rolled on top of her, clutching her hair in his hands and kissing her. They made love again, and by morning, Jason had left. Andrea rolled over, feeling the chilly side of the bed. "Good luck," she whispered.

GETTING OUT OF BED, she saw Jason's robe hanging on the door with a note in the pocket that said: *Thanks for stealing my vacation.* She grinned as she wrapped the coziness closer and wandered through the empty house. That day, she wrote a new song, dedicated to types of love. It had a jumpier beat than the other one and she felt confident that the producers would love it too.

As Jason sat on the plane to L.A. in first class, he flipped one of Andrea's guitar picks between his fingers. It stuck to his foot when he walked to the bathroom early in the night and he thought she wouldn't miss it. Across the aisle from him was a snooty-looking woman the same age as him. She eyed him as if he were a piece of meat ready to sink her teeth into him. Her eyes flashed when she saw the pick. Pushing her boobs together and hiking her tight dress, she walked over to him.

"Hey," she said in a high-pitched voice, "Are you a musician?" She fiddled with her long locks and batted her eyelashes. Before meeting Andrea, Jason enjoyed that behavior and convinced women to meet him in the bathroom. Though he still stared at her breasts and plump lips, he kept picturing how Andrea might look in a hip-hugging dress.

"No, I'm not. This belongs to my friend. I don't know if that's what I should call her."

The woman pretended to fall in his lap and giggled an apology. "She's not a great friend if she left you alone on this plane." She pushed her breasts into his face, and Jason pushed her away.

"Can you leave me alone?" he asked, "I want to rest before I get to L.A. Alone. It will be crazy enough when I get there."

She jutted out her bottom lip and attempted to put her hands on her hips. "You could use my company, Mr.

Grumpy." Her voice sounded childish, making Jason roll his eyes. He used to find it cute until he rented a cabin and met an intelligent woman. A sexy woman with a brain and a melodic voice.

"Look. My dad's dead and I'm helping my mother prepare his funeral. You're one person I need space from."

Her jaw dropped. "Oh, my God!" she squealed and clapped. "You look familiar. You're…"

"Nope. Doubt it. A million guys in California," Jason said.

"No. I just saw your picture in *The Talk*. You're that famous director's son! I knew I recognized you. I'm sorry what happened to him. I heard it was an overdose, but you can't listen to the rumors."

Jason looked over and shook his head. "Go back to your magazine and leave me alone."

"That's not nice. You need to be comforted during a time like this."

"No. What I need is for you to go away."

"I'd rather stay," she said and settled into the seat.

Jason glared at the woman. "I'd prefer you go before I call the flight attendant and he removes you to where you belong."

The lady uncrossed her legs and stood. "Well, you don't have to be so rude. I was only trying to help you through this difficult time." She sat in the open seat across the aisle and continued to ramble.

Jason stared out the window, drowning out her voice with Andrea's melodies. Seeing the city below, his chest tightened. He pressed the pick into his palm and closed his eyes, thinking of Andrea's delectable body and cheerful laugh. "Thank you, doe-eyes," he said, buckling his seatbelt as the light came on overhead.

When Andrea left the house the next day, she returned the key under the mat. Walking to the waiting driver at the end of the path, she stopped and turned. She gazed with a smile at the cabin. "If I ever return, I hope it's with him." She enjoyed the view and jumped when her phone rang.

She answered it when she saw it was her manager, Paul. "Andrea!" he exclaimed, "I've been so worried. It's been over two weeks and I've heard nothing."

"I sent you a text message."

"You did?"

"Yes."

"Well, it worried me. I wanted to send someone to rescue you," Paul said.

"Why?"

A loud breathing noise echoed through the phone. "You vanished without saying much. Then you send a quick text that looked more like something a kidnapper would send to throw detectives off the trail."

Andrea snorted. "You're being a bit dramatic, don't ya think?"

"No. Your short texts were not enough to convince me you were safe."

"I was very safe."

"And the song? We are on a deadline, Andrea."

"Getting away is what I needed," she said. "When I get back, I will play you a song that will make you proud."

"I expect nothing less than perfection from you, Andrea!"

CHAPTER NINE

AFTER ANDREA RETURNED TO CALIFORNIA, she spent time with Paul and the producers recording the song to play for Mr. Berkley, the head of the record label. Mr. Berkley made all decision on who sang any given song.

On a chilly sunny morning, Andrea bundled in a jacket met Paul at the lobby elevator of Great Hill Records. "Are you ready?"

"As ready as I've ever been," Andrea said.

They reached the eighth floor, and Paul held the elevator door to an exclusive suite and ushered her in. Behind the mahogany desk in the reception area sat a twentysomething Latino woman. She wore an off white mini-dress, red lipstick, and just the right amount of mascara to show off her shining brown eyes. "Andrea, this is Isabella Cortez," Paul said. "And Isabella, this is Andrea Walters."

Isabella gave Andrea a warm smile. "Nice to meet you."

Andrea returned the greeting.

"Is Mr. Berkley here?" Paul asked Isabella.

"He's expecting you. You might want to not ask about his day when you go in."

Paul shot a dubious look at the closed door. "It's early, how can it be that bad already?" He paused. "No time like now, Andrea."

Isabella nodded. "Good luck!"

Andrea crossed her fingers as she and Paul walked into the conference room with a waiting Mr. Berkley tapping feverously on his phone.

Andrea and Paul sat at the end of a long conference table opposite Mr. Berkley. Okay, don't panic, she told herself. You've dreamed of this moment. Should she speak? Sit? Fidget? No, definitely no fidgeting. She needed to wait for Mr. Berkley to speak first.

Paul's hand landed on Andrea's knee under the table, and she jumped up from the chair. Their eyes met and held for a moment. Relax, Andrea thought, so she returned to the chair.

Paul tilted his head and looked at her. She shrugged and mouthed *sorry.*

Mr. Berkley popped the CD into the player and pressed play. He listened, and Andrea swore she saw a smile. "I like it. It's good," he said. "Disappearing has done wonders for you, Andrea."

"Thanks," she said, looking at Paul, who exhaled louder than necessary. "I was thinking of speeding the track and releasing it online for free in a few different versions. I think if we did that, it will raise the hype for my first album."

"Album, huh?" Mr. Berkley said, straightening his tie. "You're ready for that?"

"You bet your ass, sir."

Paul coughed. He had to give Andrea credit. She was tenacious, passionate, and forthright. Hiding herself away in a cabin had helped release greatness she hadn't found. First things first. Win over Mr. Berkley. "What she means, Sir."

"I like the new Andrea, but what makes you think I haven't changed my mind?" He folded his hands.

Andrea released the breath she held. She stood, her palms pressed into the sides of the table. An image of Jason flashed across her mind. They had plastered the funeral arrangements and details of his father's life on the news. She wanted to call him, but she knew he needed space to be with his family. "Mr. Berkley," Andrea said, "over the last couple of weeks, I had an eye-opening experience. I am ready to take my career to the next level and put my heart into this album. You've said yourself that I'm an incredible songwriter. I want to be that firecracker again."

Mr. Berkley smiled. "Glad to hear it, Andrea. Get to work."

"What?! Really?!"

"Great Hills Records expects nothing but the best. We want singers that have a desire, a drive, an undeniable fire for the best. You've shown me that you have that fire."

"Thanks, Mr. Berkley," Andrea said.

"You're welcome. Now, if you don't mind, Paul and I have business to discuss," Mr. Berkley said.

Andrea nodded. She left the conference room with a smile, strutting past Isabella's desk. "He's in a better mood."

Isabella smiled.

Andrea waited until the elevator doors closed to scream and jump. The door opened again as she forgot to push a button. Two manager looking guys walked in, pretending not to notice her jumping.

Rifling through her purse, she pulled out her phone. She wanted to call Jason. *You said you'd give him space.* She dropped her phone into her purse as the elevator descended until it stopped on the lobby floor. *We did it, Hollywood.*

She inhaled while waiting for the other riders to exit before letting the air out of her lungs and stepping out of the elevator. With a spring to her step, Andrea walked through the large doors of Great Hills Records.

Crossed Up

S he had spent years avoiding them. She had spent the last five years making sure they never got close enough for those feelings inside her to turn into this. Somehow, a part of her sensed if, given a chance, placed in a situation, avoidance would be impossible.

Impossible and dangerous.

Because here she was, having kissed him once, and in love with him.

Crossed up by baseball star, Callen Moore.

"You want me?" he asked, a hint of pearly-white teeth shone through his full lips.

Yes. No. "Right here," she said. "Right now."

He closed the distance between them. She placed her palm on his chest, stretching on her painted toes, pressing her clothed body against his naked chest as she kissed him.

Callen Moore was dangerous.

He was not a guy to settle. He was a love and leave man.

She'd never thought to flirt with danger. That thought never crossed her mind. She didn't love. Relationships were out too. Megan Donahue didn't get involved. She stayed far away from baseball players—coaches—mascots and hell, the male species.

The sweat beads on his chest brushed her nipples as she arched against him. His powerful hands moved to cup her butt as he drew her up against him.

When she pulled away, she locked eyes with him. His face was flush, his eyes flaming with want. She loved looking at his need in his eyes. Enjoyed that she—Megan Donahue, the top talent scout—could cross his calculated lines.

And that he could cross her, too.

The risk was worth the potential reward.

She pulled the jersey open and kissed his Adam's apple before drifting south, pulling the jersey with her as she lowered herself until she came to kneel in front of him. Jitterbugs danced around in her stomach as she reached up and undid the button on his jeans. She could see the perfection outlined there beneath the denim.

She knew moving forward meant a greater risk. That she wouldn't be as good as any of the women he'd taken to bed. She didn't do things like this.

No one knew about the deal. No one knew what was at stake. She did.

She took her time as she lowered the zipper. Her heart, pounding in her throat as she drew the fabric of his briefs to his knees, exposing his arousal pointed at her topaz eyes.

"Megan…" His name on her lips was a warning, but she ignored.

She curled her fingers around his length, and then leaned forward, touching the tip of her tongue, tasting him.

She had never imagined herself doing this. Had never imagined wanting to, ever. She needed to make herself feel good. And she wanted…

She wanted him to remember her, to remember their moment. Despite knowing women would come after her, she wanted him to remember her.

This wasn't a loss of control. He never lost control. This was him. A man, giving in to a need.

Callen Moore got whatever he set his mind to in life. And Megan Donahue would be no different. She got what she wanted in life. And she would cross up Callen Moore's game. A dangerous game she played.

She shifted, tightening her grip on him, and seizing more of him into her mouth. And then...

The barbaric sound he made with each tap of her tongue.

The sweet flavor of him on her tongue as she proceeded to lick and suck.

He bucked his hips, and a wave of satisfaction washed over her. Satisfaction as she realized just how close he was to surrender his control. She cherished the capability to take him to the threshold. It reminded her of the way he had done the same to her in the locker room. When a kiss and a delicate stroke to her arm swung her to mush. The pull between them authentic, powerful, and indisputable.

"Megan," he rasped, his voice frayed.

"Shh," she said, "I'm enjoying myself." She received him in deeper, pleasure surging through her. Her core felt damp, an ache deepening inside her.

"You. Must. Stop. Now." He took hold of her shoulders and raised her to a standing position. "I need you. Not just... This is incredible, Meg. I need to bury myself in you. So deep I reach your spine." Suddenly he pulled her up, clutching hold of both thighs and wrapping her legs around his waist as he lay her on the bed, putting himself between her thighs. He kissed her, rocking his slick erection against that place where she was soaked and needy for him.

Thanks for reading a sneak peek of
CROSSED UP *by Susan Kiley, part of her* **Short Romance** *series!*
Available October 2018 wherever HSL Media and Susan Kiley books and eBooks are sold.
www.susanrkiley.com

SPECIAL EXCERPT FROM

Love Struck

Read on for a sneak peek of
LOVE STRUCK *by Susan Kiley, part of her* **Short
Romance** *series!*

PROLOGUE

"One song," I said over the booming music. "I need to get home."

We danced to one of my favorite songs, "Love Struck," by Travis Hunt, rising country superstar. As I danced, Travis hummed the words. My stomach felt like I'd been on a rollercoaster.

The song.

The way he hummed.

I hadn't felt topsy-turvy since… never. I'd never felt giddiness or butterflies deep inside, even with my boyfriend Brett Daly, a soccer star—no butterflies. Whatever those butterflies were doing in my body— couldn't be good—or maybe too good.

Travis's arms remained around me for a moment longer after the song had ended. At last, he released me, but with clear reluctance. "Thank you for the dance."

"I… I enjoyed it," I whispered.

We stepped apart, still gazing deep into each other's eyes. I tore my gaze from Travis's and walked away.

Brett is your boyfriend, I reminded myself while trying to focus on walking away. Everything about Travis screamed *proceed with caution. Crap! I'm love struck!*

CHAPTER ONE

"JUST ONE MORE day and summer break will be over," I said. I picked a broken seashell out of the sand and tossed it across the foamy seawater. The crisp, salty water nipped at my feet sinking in the sand as my friends basked in the scorching August midday sun. The coolness of the wet sand gave my hot shoeless feet relief. Brooke, Brett, and Jerod lounged on beach towels, while seagulls squawked as they dived in and out of the calm waters.

After throwing the seashell, plopping instead of skipping across the calm waters, I stare out into the limitless ocean. *I wish I could stay here forever.* MIT started in a week, and I wasn't looking forward to my senior year. I was, however, looking forward to my twenty-second birthday. My college friends always threw the best birthday bashes, and Brett, Jerod, and Brooke always made the trip to celebrate.

I let out a loud, exaggerated sigh. I turn to everyone. "Hey, why don't we look for shells and beach glass?

Maybe we can make a picture frame or something, to remind us of how much fun we had this summer?"

"Why don't you look, Katie, we're catching the last few days of rays before we're shuffled back to town and locked indoors at school for another nine months," said Brooke her best friend. The boys remained quiet.

"Whatever. Y'all keep getting skin cancer." My tongue jetted out of my mouth before moving down the shoreline to look for glass shards and shells. *I hate doing nothing*, keeping my eyes focused on the wet sand.

Turning to look over my shoulder, I saw I had walked quite a distance from everyone without a single shard of glass or a shell. I came upon another area of the beach, less crowded as the one my friends occupied most of the summer. As I turned around, I saw something. A sparkle in the sun. A blue-and-green piece of glass wedged into the moist sand. I bound forward as the water receded; bending to retrieve my first shard of glass.

As my fingers closed around the thick glass, a male voice yelled, "Incoming!"

It was too late.

A misfired football slammed into my head, knocking me off balance. I fell, sprawled out on my back in the moist sand, water nipping at my feet.

"Shit! I'm sorry," Crappy Catcher said.

I stare up at a tanned, freckled face boy shielding the sun. I shake my head before I push myself to a sitting position, sand falling from my hair onto my sandy legs. I ignore the extended hand and bound to my feet. My angry hazel eyes shielded by my now catty-wampus sunglasses.

"Miles of beach and your friend throws it here," I said. Turning with open arms, "Right here where I've found the only glass shard on the dang beach." I remove the lopsided glasses and stare at the smirking dark-haired, handsome boy. He slides his glasses down his nose—hazel meets sky-blue eyes.

Pushing the glasses back into the position he reaches down and grabs the football lodged into the sand.

"I guess he wanted me to meet you," he said. He grinned and wiggled his brows at me.

Is he flirting with me? He knocked me on my butt, broke my sunglasses and now—what, he's trying to pick me up at the beach? The nerve!

My hand instinctively flew to my forehead. A small lump had popped through the skin. "Oww," I said.

"Hey, I am sorry. That's gonna leave a mark. Are you okay?"

"Yeah. I'm sure I'll live, unlike my glasses," I mumble. Less angry with the hazel eyes penetrating my angry exterior, I remember the glass shard. Turning, I look down and see the twinkling glass, threatening to leave with the water receding into the ocean.

"Are you good?" Crappy Catcher said. He moved two steps closer to Katie.

"Glass. There. Grab it," I said, bolting to my right, "*OOMPH!*" Slamming my body into him, knocking us both off balance and into the wet sand. This time, face down on top of the smoking hot body. My sky-blue eyes met his hazel eyes as our sunglasses go flying from the force of our bodies tumbling in the sand.

"We gotta stop meeting like this," he said.

"As if! You did this… You. Again."

"Me? You are the one —"

"You are the one who moved forward as I tried picking up the piece of glass," I said.

"I'd say it worked out in my favor then, wouldn't you?" he wiggled his eyes.

"How do you figure?"

"From my perspective," he wiggled his brows again. "I seem to have the best place on the beach."

"How... Oh shit!" I was still laying on top of him. I quickly pushed with my hands against his—nice and tight chest—until I was standing. He, remained on his back, staring up at me.

"Sorry. I'm done looking for today," I said. I could feel my face getting hot.

"What? Do you need your glass?"

"No."

"There's plenty of sun and beach. Want help?" he asked.

Looking back over my shoulders down the beach at my friends still laying on their beach towels with no interest in helping, she replies, "Sure, why not." She turns back toward him, letting out a sigh. *What'll Brett think? Who cares, he's too busy getting cancer to care about what I like. Have fun Katie, it's your last day, and he's way cute!*

He found himself on her left side ankle deep in water as they strode down the beach in search of glass shards. "What do you do with all the glass?" he asked.

"Put it in a box." I tried to keep my eyes on the wet sand and not on the hard body next to me.

He raised his hands in a surrender gesture. "Okay, we got off to a bad start. My name is T-Travis Johnson. My friends call me Travis."

I cock a brow.

"I know, makes little sense," he said.

My head tilts to the left.

I stop.

I turn to my left and stick my sandy hand out. He stops, turns, and squeezes my hand. "I'm Katie Larson, and this is my last day." In a strained voice I added, "I've got a boyfriend."

Sometimes I didn't feel like I had a boyfriend, Brett Johnson. Everyone knew Brett as the popular boy in high school—he picked me three years ago. I looked at Travis to see his reaction. He didn't blink, smile, frown, or show he cared either way. I smiled. Butterflies sprang to life inside my body, reacting to his intoxicating stare.

A familiar stare. I'd seen the stare before, somewhere but could not place it.

He gave a toothy grin. "You want to go get a Sno cone?"

I blinked. The butterflies in an all-out war inside my body surprised me. I could feel my face warming under the closeness of Travis and the melodic tone of his voice. She shook her head. "I should get back. My friends are looking for me." *Doubtful.*

"Some other time then," Travis said. He reached into his board shorts and retrieved his cell phone. "Can I get your number?"

I rolled my bottom lip between my teeth contemplating if giving him my number was a good idea. A few more punches from the butterflies inside my belly. "Yeah, sure. Give me your phone."

He looked down at the phone after I gave it back. I bit my bottom lip again.

"I'd stop biting your lip like that," Travis said.

"Oh, sorry. It's a nervous habit," I said quickly turning on my heels and heading down the beach toward my friends.

"But—" he tried calling out, but I was too far away. I could feel his intense stare as I pick up the pace. My long, and lean legs carried my athletic body through the wet sand hurrying back to my friends. I stop for a moment, turning over my shoulder to catch one last glimpse of Travis. He and his friends had returned to playing catch with their football.

Once I'd made it back to Brett's beach house, I stand at the bottom of the stairs and take two deep breaths before ascending and joining my friends.

CHAPTER TWO

"WELL, WELL. DID YOU enjoy your glass hunt?" Brooke said without looking up from her magazine.

"Eh. Waste of time," I said.

Brooke placed the magazine on her lap and looked up, making direct eye contact with Me. "A total waste of time?"

I worked hard to contain the smile when I thought of Travis. "Yup."

"Brett's pissed. You were on the beach for an hour." Brooke looked over her shoulder checking to see if he was anywhere within earshot. "I saw you with a certain hottie way over there on the beach."

"What's new. He increased his risk of cancer than doing something I wanted to do," I said in a flat tone. I plopped down in the chair next to Brooke and stared out over the beach and into the calm ocean waters.

Brooked turned to face me. "Tell me about him, the cute boy," Brooke bounced in her seat, sending her magazine tumbling to the ground.

I looked at my best friend with my sky-blue eyes. "Butterflies."

"Butterflies? What does that mean?" Brooke asked.

"I have these weird feelings inside my body. I don't get them when I'm around Brett. Ever."

Brooke scooted closer and shook her head as though confused and excited for me. "Ooh, like dancing butterflies or a throbbing where your heart is about to come out of your chest?"

"Um-mm."

"And your knees feel weak like you will fall to the ground?"

"Yes. Like—" Brooke interrupted my thought.

"Like you're in love?!" Brooke said too loud as I placed a hand over her mouth to shush her.

"Yes. I mean no. I mean, I don't know. I don't know what love feels like," I said removing my hand from Brooke's mouth and looking out over the ocean. "I've never felt like this before. Love I guess."

Brooke shook her head again, grabbing the magazine off the ground and adjusting herself in the chair. "You know, there's an entire world that'd love to have Brett Johnson as their boyfriend. I'd be careful if I were you.

You never know who may come along and snatch him up," she said as she raised the magazine back in front of her face.

"And? Would that be a bad thing?" I smiled thinking about Travis. I liked the look of his body, the way his face lit up when he spoke, and how he made butterflies dance in her body.

"Wait. You'd let someone else have him, just like that?" Brooke asked. "How many times did you wish he'd ask you on a date? Now he's yours; you act like it's nothing. Like he's chop liver because Mr. Hottie can't catch a football."

I knew Brooke was right. I was not about to tell her I agreed. I wanted to date Brett ever since the fifth grade. I'd write Mrs. Johnson on every piece of paper, and every night, I'd wish upon the brightest star that Brett would ask me to be his girlfriend. On the last day of our senior year, he asked me to be his girlfriend. He was the most popular and good-looking boy in the school. *I should be happy.*

"Well, it's not like I'll ever see him again. Our summer is over, and I'm leaving for my internship." My eyes return to the beach searching for a glimpse of Travis.

"Hey, the food's here! Get it while it's hot," Brett yells from inside the house.

Jarod, Brooke's on-again-off-again boyfriend appears behind Brooke holding a barbecue chicken wing.

I turn around and threw a smile toward Brett and Jarod. "Be there in a second," I said.

"Better hurry buttercup or Jarod will eat it all," Brett said. He made a fist and gave Jarod a playful punch in the arm.

"Crap! He will, too." Brooke threw the magazine on the small table between us and jumped to her feet and ran into the house.

I shook my head and followed everyone into the house. Brooke was a petite, short girl with an appetite of a football linebacker.

Jarod chuckled with a full mouth of chicken. "I like food. If you think about it, I'm helping you girls."

"How do you figure?" I asked reaching for a slice of pizza.

Jarod grabs the largest slice in the box. "You see this right here? It's bad. Fattening," Jarod said. "It goes to those hips." He points the pizza at Brooke's hips. "And that is no good."

Brooke cocks an eyebrow at Jarod, "Who says?" she asks. "Why can't girls have larger hips?"

"Says the girl who has no hips," I spit out through a full mouth.

"All I'm saying is… girls can eat whatever they like, and look however they want. If it should concern anyone," grabbing another slice of pizza, "is you, Jarod. You packed on the hip pounds this summer," Brooke teased.

Jarod shrugged. He looked down at his bare belly hanging over the waist of his trunks and rubs it. "Buddha belly means good luck in some cultures. Wanna rub my belly?"

Brooke picked up her third slice of pizza. "Nah, I'm good. Besides, I'm not the one who needs the luck."

I stop mid bite.

Brett laughs and rubs his washboard stomach. "Not everyone can have good genetics like me. Jarod's a growing boy, and he needs to eat. Besides, the heavier he is, the better he can block for me this year."

Brooke and I looked at each other and rolled our eyes. I grabbed a can of Barq's and retreated to a seat outside, staring into the ocean. Brett followed taking the position next to mine.

I glanced over at Brett. He was good-looking; brown eyes and short sandy blonde hair. He was popular. He had laid the path for a future of fame and fortune. Brett didn't give her the butterflies as Travis did. My eyes returned to the ocean and a nearby group running around in the sand. I wondered if Travis was one, waiting for another clumsy girl to rescue.

Travis differed from Brett and all the boys she'd known all her life. He had sandy blonde hair that was shorter and coal-like eyes. I couldn't stop thinking about how he looked at me. For a moment, I felt like the only girl on the beach and the universe. He was a light and I am mosquito drawn to him.

"What's on your mind, Katie? You've been staring out over the ocean." He reached over and touched my arm with his fingers.

I pulled my arm away and wrapped it around my waist. I wanted Travis's touch, not Brett's. "Nothing," I lied.

"Come on. It's me. What's bothering you?" Brett asked. His blue eyes showed concern.

I said, "No. I wish…"

"Cool," Brett said without letting me finish my sentence. He turned toward Jerod, who was taking a sip of his soda and chewing pizza. "Let's go for a ride, Crush."

"Hell yes!" Jerod said. He gulped the remaining contents of the can and slammed it onto the coffee table.

"Have fun," I said.

"Oh, come on. Don't be a fun sponge," Brett said.

"Nah, not feeling it tonight."

Brett pushed his bottom lip out and gave his best puppy-dog eye expression.

I shook my head. "I'm heading out. I've had enough fun for one day." The last thing I wanted to do was go for a ride with Brett. I wanted another chance encounter with Travis. I didn't want to leave and miss a chance of seeing the boy who gave me butterflies.

CHAPTER THREE

I DROVE MY car into the driveway of my parent's house, turned the radio up a few notches as my favorite new song, *Love Struck*, by Travis Hunt, blared and parked. As the song ended, I switched off the ignition and walked to the front door, allowing my feet to drag my slapping sandals against the hot cement of the walkway.

"Hello, anyone home," I yelled out as I dropped my keys and sandy purse on the floor next to the hall table. I shift through the house and transfer my phone from one salty palm to the other making my way to the back patio.

Laughter and splashing roll through the quiet space of the house.

The thing is, I wish I had a reason to stay. Instead, my summer break is almost over and must return to my last year at MIT. Staying in one place for long is boring, unadventurous. For most of my life, I had the same unadventurous and dreary summer. But on those rare occasions, someone invited me on a spring or Christmas break; I wanted to leave. I can't win.

"Katie! Katie! Watch me," Colton said. He dove into the pool, or rather belly-flopped.

"Looks like you've been practicing, Colton. What are you doing in the pool by yourself?"

Colton swam to the side of the pool. "Grams' here."

I do a quick scan of the yard. "I don't see Grams, Colton."

"Katie! I'm so glad you're home," came the sweet elderly voice of Grams. "Do you think you can keep an eye on Colton while I go run an errand?"

"Of course," I say giving Grams a quick hug before she was through the kitchen door and out of sight.

I turn and head straight for the pool. "Ready or not, here I come!" I took a flying leap into the pool–cannonball style. When I came up for air, I shot a mouthful of chlorinated water at my little brother. Not that Colton was little, he was sixteen but had Asperger's.

Colton cupped his hands and splashed water in my direction. A water fight ensued. We continued until Colton turned on his back and floated to the deep end of the pool. I looked at the dancing clouds and wondered about Travis.

"Earth to Katie," Colton screamed from the other end of the pool, "Let's race." He was in the starting position against the wall in the deep end.

I shook the daydream from my mind and smiled at Colton.

"You got it. I hate winning every time we race."

"Whatever. You cheat. That's how you win," Colton said.

I took my position next to Colton with a sly smile and a quick wink before he yelled, "Go!"

"Hey, that's not fair," I yelled, trying to sound angry. I take off after Colton.

"I win!" Colton screamed while splashing the water in celebration.

I shake my head. "I let you win after you cheated."

"Poor sport, Katie. I won, and you lost."

I opened my arms wide on top of the water and in one quick coming together motion, sent water hurling toward Colton, soaking every wet spot on his six-foot body. As the water settled, I climbed out of the pool. "Are you done yet? You're turning into a raisin." I knew he'd stay in the water all day if allowed. She grabbed one of the oversized beach towels from the chairs and threw it at Colton as he emerged from the pool.

I spread one towel out on one of the lawn chairs, the other wrapped around my long hair before covering my eyes with an oversized black pair of sunglasses. Yawning, I close my eyes and think about Travis.

Thirty minutes later, I woke just as Grams came out of the house.

"Katie, your phone is buzzing in the kitchen," Grams said. Her heavy feet in her flip-flop sandals smacked the concrete patio as she walked.

I sprung to my feet letting the towel covering my hair fall to the ground. I darted into the kitchen to retrieve the buzzing phone. "Thanks, Grams."

Grams smiled. I returned to the lawn chair next to the pool dialing Brett's number.

"Hey," I said into the phone. I listened as Brett asked me to go with him, Jerod, and Brooke to a movie. I said I didn't think it would be a problem but wanted to see what Grams and Colton had planned for the night. Brett waited on the phone. I walked across the patio and into the kitchen to ask Grams if she cared. She nodded.

"I can go," I said into the phone to Brett. "Seven-thirty? Okay, I'll be ready." I pushed the end button and laid it on the counter in the kitchen.

"What movie are you going to see, honey?" Grams asked. She stopped preparing dinner for a moment to lock eyes with Katie. Then, she smiled.

"Love, Simon," I answered. I reached for a glass to pour myself fresh lemonade Grams had made earlier in the day.

"I heard a few reviews on the television the other day, sounds like a great movie," Grams said before returning to her preparation. "Did you have fun today?"

I nodded, though Grams wasn't looking. "I was over at Brett's beach house. Jerod and Brooke were there, too. We didn't do much. There were many people on the beach."

"Oh, that sounds lovely, dear." Grams rumple-skinned hand brushed a stray gray hair away from her nose. "How's Brett doing?"

I sipped my lemonade and didn't want to talk about Brett. I tried to tell Grams about Travis. Brett liked talking about all the people he met during his soccer games, endorsement parties, and team functions. I didn't care about all that. I preferred simplicity.

"I need to take a shower before dinner."

As I left the kitchen, I heard Grams mutter something about 'Brett is such a sweet young boy' and 'Katie is hiding something.' I wasn't hiding anything, except that I met an amazing down-to-earth boy, Travis.

I knew Grams didn't know much about Brett, or at least she didn't lead onto knowing much about Brett and how every girl ogled over him and every boy wanted to be him. Brett liked the paparazzi and having his photo taken. I preferred staying out of the flashing of the cameras and screaming fans. Brett has everything. *So, how come I can't stop thinking about Travis?*

Thanks for reading a sneak peek of
LOVE STRUCK *by Susan Kiley, part of her* **Short Romance** *series!*
Available September 2018 wherever HSL Media and Susan Kiley books and eBooks are sold.
www.susanrkiley.com

Searing pages leaving readers wanting more, no one does it like

SUSAN KILEY

Grab a glass of wine.
Sexy characters and sweet kisses are waiting.
Order you copies now!

****To receive an exclusive FREE BOOK and an alert when Susan's next book releases, go to www.susanrkiley.com and subscribe****

ACKNOWLEDGMENTS

Thank you to all my amazing readers who asked me to write more short stories. I started with Love Struck because the characters were sweet, and I'm happy Katie and Travis bumped into one another on the beach. Their story is far from over…

Cabin Fever reminds me of times when a person need to get away and find themselves—so thank you Andrea and Jason.

Big hugs to my manuscript's first readers—you know who you are. ☺ Your feedback and support means the world to me. I love adding fans to the ARC list, so if you'd like added, please email me.

As always, mucho hugs to my three amazing children who hear the tapping of keys late in the night while I'm trying to finish another story. You all inspire me to keep writing and living my dreams. One day, you'll be old enough to read my stories. You guys rock! Love you guys! XO

AFTERWORD

Thank you for purchasing my book. I sincerely hope you enjoyed it! As an author, your **Ratings and Reviews** are extremely important to me! I would appreciate it if you would take the time to award a star rating and/or write a short review (a sentence or two) on how reading my book made you feel.

Please rate/review on Amazon. If you are a member of Goodreads, you may rate me over on that site too. ☺

I value my readers dearly and would love to stay connected!

Please follow me on social media:
Facebook @susanrkiley
Twitter @susanrkiley
Instagram @susanrkiley
Pinterest @susanrkiley

Subscribe and be the first to get new release information, sneak peaks, latest news and more! Visit my website, **www.susanrkiley.com** and fill out the **subscribe** form.

Should you wish to personally be in touch with me, you may email me at **susan@susanrkiley.com**

ABOUT THE AUTHOR

An emerging author in Romance Fiction, Young Readers, and in the Motivational and Self-Help genres, Susan's inspiration for her books emanate from her keen interest in all things romantic. From flowers, wine, and second chances to picturesque landscapes and warm snuggles during snow storms in the Midwest.

As a mother of three, she stands little to no chance. Romance often includes children vying for couch space, cleaning soiled uniforms, or reminding one of the boys to put the seat down so their sister doesn't fall in.

Her insatiable lust for romance regularly propels her to take mini-getaways to picturesque places in the Midwest. Besides traveling, she loves Frisbee golf and coaching volleyball. She holds fast to the idea that love at first sight and second chances at love do exist.

SUSAN KILEY, a freelance editor for traditional and self-publishers since 2005, opened HSL Media, an international book-editing company (**www.heartstrongpublishing.com**), and an online writer's course company (**www.writerscrashcourse.com**). She is a contributing writer and editor at **www.content-stylist.com**.

Susan writes in her home in rural Iowa, and online at **www.susanrkiley.com**.